A Drama on the Seashore

Rhonda Mohammed

colouring
CLASSICS

A Drama on the Seashore

N early all young men have a compass with which they delight in measuring the future. When their will is equal to the breadth of the angle at which they open it the world is theirs. But this phenomenon of the inner life takes place only at a certain age. That age, which for all men lies between twenty-two and twenty-eight, is the period of great thoughts, of fresh conceptions, because it is the age of immense desires. After that age, short as the seed-time, comes that of execution. There are, as it were, two youths,—the youth of belief, the youth of action; these are often commingled in men whom Nature has favored and who, like Caesar, like Newton, like Bonaparte, are the greatest among great men.

I was measuring how long a time it might take a thought to develop. Compass in hand, standing on a rock some hundred fathoms above the ocean, the waves of which were breaking on the reef below, I surveyed my future, filling it with books as an engineer or builder traces on vacant ground a palace or a fort.

The sea was beautiful; I had just dressed after bathing; and I awaited Pauline, who was also bathing, in a granite cove floored with fine sand, the most coquettish bath-room that Nature ever devised for her water-fairies. The spot was at the farther end of Croisic, a dainty little peninsula in Brittany; it was far from the port, and so inaccessible that the coast-guard seldom thought it necessary to pass that way. To float in ether after floating on the wave!—ah! who would not have floated on the future as I did! Why was I thinking? Whence comes evil?—who knows! Ideas drop into our hearts or into our heads without consulting us. No courtesan was ever more capricious nor more imperious than conception is to artists; we must grasp it, like fortune, by the hair when it comes.

Astride upon my thought, like Astolphe on his hippogriff, I was galloping through worlds, suiting them to my fancy. Presently, as I looked about me to find some omen for the bold productions my wild imagination was urging me to undertake, a pretty cry, the cry of a woman issuing refreshed and joyous from a bath, rose above the murmur of the rippling fringes as their flux and reflux marked a white line along the shore. Hearing that note as it gushed from a soul, I fancied I saw among the rocks the foot of an angel, who with outspread wings cried out to me, "Thou shalt succeed!" I came down radiant, light-hearted; I bounded like a pebble rolling down a rapid slope. When she saw me, she said,—

"What is it?"

I did not answer; my eyes were moist. The night before, Pauline had understood my sorrows, as she now understood my joy, with the magical sensitiveness of a harp that obeys the variations of the atmosphere. Human life has glorious moments. Together we walked in silence along the beach. The sky was cloudless, the sea without a ripple; others might have thought them merely two blue surfaces, the one above the other, but we—we who heard without the need of words, we who could evoke between these two infinitudes the illusions that nourish youth, —we pressed each other's hands at every change in the sheet of water or the sheets of air, for we took those slight phenomena as the visible translation of our double thought. Who has never tasted in wedded love that moment of illimitable joy when the soul seems freed from the trammels of flesh, and finds itself restored, as it were, to the world whence it came? Are there not hours when feelings clasp each other and fly upward, like children taking hands and running, they scarce know why? It was thus we went along.

At the moment when the village roofs began to show like a faint gray line on the horizon, we met a fisherman, a poor man returning to Croisic. His feet were bare; his linen trousers ragged round the bottom; his shirt of common sailcloth, and his jacket tatters. This abject poverty pained us; it was like a discord amid our harmonies. We looked at each other, grieving mutually that we had not at that moment the power to dip into the treasury of Aboul Casem. But we saw a splendid lobster and a crab fastened to a string which the fisherman was dangling in his right hand, while with the left he held his tackle and his net.

We accosted him with the intention of buying his haul,—an idea which came to us both, and was expressed in a smile, to which I responded by a slight pressure of the arm I held and drew toward my heart. It was one of those nothings of which memory makes poems when we sit by the fire and recall the hour when that nothing moved us, and the place where it did so,—a mirage the effects of which have never been noted down, though it appears on the objects that surround us in moments when life sits lightly and our hearts are full. The loveliest scenery is that we make ourselves. What man with any poesy in him does not remember some mere mass of rock, which holds, it may be, a greater place in his memory than the celebrated landscapes of other lands, sought at great cost. Beside that rock, tumultuous thoughts! There a whole life evolved; there all fears dispersed; there the rays of hope descended to the soul! At this moment, the sun, sympathizing with these thoughts of love and of the future, had cast an ardent glow upon the savage flanks of the rock; a few wild mountain flowers were visible; the stillness and the silence magnified that rugged pile,— really sombre, though tinted by the dreamer, and beautiful beneath its scanty vegetation, the warm chamomile, the Venus' tresses with their velvet leaves. Oh, lingering festival; oh, glorious decorations; oh, happy exaltation of human forces! Once already the lake of Brienne had spoken to me thus. The rock of Croisic may be perhaps the last of these my joys. If so, what will become of Pauline?

"Have you had a good catch to-day, my man?" I said to the fisherman.

"Yes, monsieur," he replied, stopping and turning toward us the swarthy face of those who spend whole days exposed to the reflection of the sun upon the water.

That face was an emblem of long resignation, of the patience of a fisherman and his quiet ways. The man had a voice without harshness, kind lips, evidently no ambition, and something frail and puny about him. Any other sort of countenance would, at that moment, have jarred upon us.

"Where shall you sell your fish?"

"In the town."

"How much will they pay you for that lobster?"

"Fifteen sous."

"And the crab?"

"Twenty sous."

"Why so much difference between a lobster and a crab?"

"Monsieur, the crab is much more delicate eating. Besides, it's as malicious as a monkey, and it seldom lets you catch it."

"Will you let us buy the two for a hundred sous?" asked Pauline.

The man seemed petrified.

"You shall not have it!" I said to her, laughing. "I'll pay ten francs; we should count the emotions in."

"Very well," she said, "then I'll pay ten francs, two sous."

"Ten francs, ten sous."

"Twelve francs."

"Fifteen francs."

"Fifteen francs, fifty centimes," she said.

"One hundred francs."

"One hundred and fifty francs."

I yielded. We were not rich enough at that moment to bid higher. Our poor fisherman did not know whether to be angry at a hoax, or to go mad with joy; we drew him from his quandary by giving him the name of our landlady and telling him to take the lobster and the crab to her house.

"Do you earn enough to live on?" I asked the man, in order to discover the cause of his evident penury.

"With great hardships, and always poorly," he replied. "Fishing on the coast, when one hasn't a boat or deep-sea nets, nothing but pole and line, is a very uncertain business. You see we have to wait for the fish, or the shell-fish; whereas a real fisherman puts out to sea for them. It is so hard to earn a living this way that I'm the only man in these parts who fishes along-shore. I spend whole days without getting anything. To catch a crab, it must go to sleep, as this one did, and a lobster must be silly enough to stay among the rocks. Sometimes after a high tide the mussels come in and I grab them."

"Well, taking one day with another, how much do you earn?"

"Oh, eleven or twelve sous. I could do with that if I were alone; but I have got my old father to keep, and he can't do anything, the good man, because he's blind."

At these words, said simply, Pauline and I looked at each other without a word; then I asked,—

"Haven't you a wife, or some good friend?"

He cast upon us one of the most lamentable glances that I ever saw as he answered,—

"If I had a wife I must abandon my father; I could not feed him and a wife and children too."

"Well, my poor lad, why don't you try to earn more at the salt marshes, or by carrying the salt to the harbor?"

"Ah, monsieur, I couldn't do that work three months. I am not strong enough, and if I died my father would have to beg. I am forced to take a business which only needs a little knack and a great deal of patience."

"But how can two persons live on twelve sous a day?"

"Oh, monsieur, we eat cakes made of buckwheat, and barnacles which I get off the rocks."

"How old are you?"

"Thirty-seven."

"Did you ever leave Croisic?"

5

"I went once to Guerande to draw for the conscription; and I went to Savenay to the messieurs who measure for the army. If I had been half an inch taller they'd have made me a soldier. I should have died of my first march, and my poor father would to-day be begging his bread."

I had thought out many dramas; Pauline was accustomed to great emotions beside a man so suffering as myself; well, never had either of us listened to words so moving as these. We walked on in silence, measuring, each of us, the silent depths of that obscure life, admiring the nobility of a devotion which was ignorant of itself. The strength of that feebleness amazed us; the man's unconscious generosity belittled us. I saw that poor being of instinct chained to that rock like a galley-slave to his ball; watching through twenty years for shell-fish to earn a living, and sustained in his patience by a single sentiment. How many hours wasted on a lonely shore! How many hopes defeated by a change of weather! He was hanging there to a granite rock, his arm extended like that of an Indian fakir, while his father, sitting in their hovel, awaited, in silence and darkness, a meal of the coarsest bread and shell-fish, if the sea permitted.

"Do you ever drink wine?" I asked.

"Three or four times a year," he replied.

"Well, you shall drink it to-day,—you and your father; and we will send you some white bread."

"You are very kind, monsieur."

"We will give you your dinner if you will show us the way along the shore to Batz, where we wish to see the tower which overlooks the bay between Batz and Croisic."

"With pleasure," he said. "Go straight before you, along the path you are now on, and I will follow you when I have put away my tackle."

We nodded consent, and he ran off joyfully toward the town. This meeting maintained us in our previous mental condition; but it lessened our gay lightheartedness.

"Poor man!" said Pauline, with that accent which removes from the compassion of a woman all that is mortifying in human pity, "ought we not to feel ashamed of our happiness in presence of such misery?"

"Nothing is so cruelly painful as to have powerless desires," I answered. "Those two poor creatures, the father and son, will never know how keen our sympathy for them is, any more than the world will know how beautiful are their lives; they are laying up their treasures in heaven."

"Oh, how poor this country is!" she said, pointing to a field enclosed by a dry stone wall, which was covered with droppings of cow's dung applied symmetrically. "I asked a peasant-woman who was busy sticking them on, why it was done; she answered that she was making fuel. Could you have imagined that when those patches of dung have dried, human beings would collect them, store them, and use them for fuel? During the winter, they are even sold as peat is sold. And what do you suppose the best dressmaker in the place can earn?—five sous a day!" adding, after a pause, "and her food."

"But see," I said, "how the winds from the sea bend or destroy everything. There are no trees. Fragments of wreckage or old vessels that are broken up are sold to those who can afford to buy; for costs of transportation are too heavy to allow them to use the firewood with which Brittany abounds. This region is fine for none but noble souls; persons without sentiments could never live here; poets and barnacles alone should inhabit it. All that ever brought a population to this rock were the salt-marshes and the factory which prepares the salt. On one side the sea; on the other, sand; above, illimitable space."

We had now passed the town, and had reached the species of desert which separates Croisic from the village of Batz. Imagine, my dear uncle, a barren track of miles covered with the glittering sand of the seashore. Here and there a few rocks lifted their heads; you might have thought them gigantic animals couchant on the dunes. Along the coast were reefs, around which the water foamed and sparkled, giving them the appearance of great white roses, floating on the liquid surface or resting on the shore. Seeing this barren tract with the ocean on one side, and on the other the arm of the sea which runs up between Croisic and the rocky shore of Guerande, at the base of which lay the salt marshes, denuded of vegetation, I looked at Pauline and asked her if she felt the courage to face the burning sun and the strength to walk through sand.

"I have boots," she said. "Let us go," and she pointed to the tower of Batz, which arrested the eye by its immense pile placed there like a pyramid; but a slender, delicately outlined pyramid, a pyramid so poetically ornate that the imagination figured in it the earliest ruin of a great Asiatic city.

We advanced a few steps and sat down upon the portion of a large rock which was still in the shade. But it was now eleven o'clock, and the shadow, which ceased at our feet, was disappearing rapidly.

"How beautiful this silence!" she said to me; "and how the depth of it is deepened by the rhythmic quiver of the wave upon the shore."

"If you will give your understanding to the three immensities which surround us, the water, the air, and the sands, and listen exclusively to the repeating sounds of flux and reflux," I answered her, "you will not be able to endure their speech; you will think it is uttering a thought which will annihilate you. Last evening, at sunset, I had that sensation; and it exhausted me."

"Oh! let us talk, let us talk," she said, after a long pause. "I understand it. No orator was ever more terrible. I think," she continued, presently, "that I perceive the causes of the harmonies which surround us. This landscape, which has but three marked colors, —the brilliant yellow of the sands, the blue of the sky, the even green of the sea,—is grand without being savage; it is immense, yet not a desert; it is monotonous, but it does not weary; it has only three elements, and yet it is varied."

"Women alone know how to render such impressions," I said. "You would be the despair of a poet, dear soul that I divine so well!"

"The extreme heat of mid-day casts into those three expressions of the infinite an all-powerful color," said Pauline, smiling. "I can here conceive the poesy and the passion of the East."

"And I can perceive its despair."

"Yes," she said, "this dune is a cloister,—a sublime cloister."

We now heard the hurried steps of our guide; he had put on his Sunday clothes. We addressed a few ordinary words to him; he seemed to think that our mood had changed, and with that reserve that comes of misery, he kept silence. Though from time to time we pressed each other's hands that we might feel the mutual flow of our ideas and impressions, we walked along for half an hour in silence, either because we were oppressed by the heat which rose in waves from the burning sands, or because the difficulty of walking absorbed our attention. Like children, we held each other's hands; in fact, we could hardly have made a dozen steps had we walked arm in arm. The path which led to Batz was not so much as traced. A gust of wind was enough to efface all tracks left by the hoofs of horses or the wheels of carts; but the practised eye of our guide could recognize by scraps of mud or the dung of cattle the road that crossed that desert, now descending towards the sea, then rising landward according to either the fall of the ground or the necessity of rounding some breastwork of rock. By mid-day, we were only half way.

"We will stop to rest over there," I said, pointing to a promontory of rocks sufficiently high to make it probable we should find a grotto.

The fisherman, who heard me and saw the direction in which I pointed, shook his head, and said,—

"Some one is there. All those who come from the village of Batz to Croisic, or from Croisic to Batz, go round that place; they never pass it."

These words were said in a low voice, and seemed to indicate a mystery.

"Who is he,—a robber, a murderer?"

Our guide answered only by drawing a deep breath, which redoubled our curiosity.

"But if we pass that way, would any harm happen to us?"

"Oh, no!"

"Will you go with us?"

"No, monsieur."

"We will go, if you assure us there is no danger."

"I do not say so," replied the fisherman, hastily. "I only say that he who is there will say nothing to you, and do you no harm. He never so much as moves from his place."

"Who is it?"

"A man."

Never were two syllables pronounced in so tragic a manner. At this moment we were about fifty feet from the rocky eminence, which extended a long reef into the sea. Our guide took a path which led him round the base of the rock. We ourselves continued our way over it; but Pauline took my arm. Our guide hastened his steps in order to meet us on the other side, where the two paths came together again.

This circumstance excited our curiosity, which soon became so keen that our hearts were beating as if with a sense of fear. In spite of the heat of the day, and the fatigue caused by toiling through the sand, our souls were still surrendered to the softness unspeakable of our exquisite ecstasy. They were filled with that pure pleasure which cannot be described unless we liken it to the joy of listening to enchanting music, Mozart's "Audiamo mio ben," for instance. When two pure sentiments blend together, what is that but two sweet voices singing? To be able to appreciate properly the emotion that held us, it would be necessary to share the state of half sensuous delight into which the events of the morning had plunged us. Admire for a long time some pretty dove with iridescent colors, perched on a swaying branch above a spring, and you will give a cry of pain when you see a hawk swooping down upon her, driving its steel claws into her breast, and bearing her away with murderous rapidity. When we had advanced a step or two into an open space which lay before what seemed to be a grotto, a sort of esplanade placed a hundred feet above the ocean, and protected from its fury by buttresses of rock, we suddenly experienced an electrical shudder, something resembling the shock of a sudden noise awaking us in the dead of night.

We saw, sitting on a vast granite boulder, a man who looked at us. His glance, like that of the flash of a cannon, came from two bloodshot eyes, and his stoical immobility could be compared only to the immutable granite masses that surrounded him. His eyes moved slowly, his body remaining rigid as though he were petrified. Then, having cast upon us that look which struck us like a blow, he turned his eyes once more to the limitless ocean, and gazed upon it, in spite of its dazzling light, as eagles gaze at the sun, without lowering his eyelids. Try to remember, dear uncle, one of those old oaks, whose knotty trunks, from which the branches have been lopped, rise with weird power in some lonely place, and you will have an image of this man. Here was a ruined Herculean frame, the face of an Olympian Jove, destroyed by age, by hard sea toil, by grief, by common food, and blackened as it were by lightning. Looking at his hard and hairy hands, I saw that the sinews stood out like cords of iron. Everything about him denoted strength of constitution. I noticed in a corner of the grotto a quantity of moss, and on a sort of ledge carved by nature on the granite, a loaf of bread, which covered the mouth of an earthenware jug. Never had my imagination, when it carried me to the deserts where early Christian anchorites spent their lives, depicted to my mind a form more grandly religious nor more horribly repentant than that of this man. You, who have a life-long experience of the confessional, dear uncle, you may never, perhaps, have seen so awful a remorse,—remorse sunk in the waves of prayer, the ceaseless supplication of a mute despair. This fisherman, this mariner, this hard, coarse Breton, was sublime through some hidden emotion. Had those eyes wept? That hand, moulded for an unwrought statue, had it struck? That ragged brow, where savage honor was imprinted, and on which strength had left vestiges of the gentleness which is an attribute of all true strength, that forehead furrowed with wrinkles, was it in harmony with the heart within? Why was this man in the granite? Why was the granite in the man? Which was the man, which was the granite? A world of fancies came into our minds. As our guide had prophesied, we passed in silence, rapidly; when he met us he saw our emotion of mingled terror and astonishment, but he made no boast of the truth of his prediction; he merely said,—

"You have seen him."

"Who is that man?"

"They call him the Man of the Vow."

You can imagine the movement with which our two heads turned at once to our guide. He was a simple-hearted fellow; he understood at once our mute inquiry, and here follows what he told us; I shall try to give it as best I can in his own language, retaining his popular parlance.

"Madame, folks from Croisic and those from Batz think this man is guilty of something, and is doing a penance ordered by a famous rector to whom he confessed his sin somewhere beyond Nantes. Others think that Cambremer, that's his name, casts an evil fate on those who come within his air, and so they always look which way the wind is before they pass this rock. If it's nor'-westerly they wouldn't go by, no, not if their errand was to get a bit of the true cross; they'd go back, frightened. Others—they are the rich folks of Croisic—they say that Cambremer has made a vow, and that's why people call him the Man of the Vow. He is there night and day, he never leaves the place. All these sayings have some truth in them. See there," he continued, turning round to show us a thing we had not remarked, "look at that wooden cross he has set up there, to the left, to show that he has put himself under the protection of God and the holy Virgin and the saints. But the fear that people have of him keeps him as safe as if he were guarded by a troop of soldiers. He has never said one word since he locked himself up in the open air in this way; he lives on bread and water, which is brought to him every morning by his brother's daughter, a little lass about twelve years old to whom he has left his property, a pretty creature, gentle as a lamb, a nice little girl, so pleasant. She has such blue eyes, long as THAT," he added, marking a line on his thumb, "and hair like the cherubim. When you ask her: 'Tell me, Perotte' (That's how we say Pierette in these parts," he remarked, interrupting himself; "she is vowed to Saint Pierre; Cambremer is named Pierre, and he was her godfather)—'Tell me, Perotte, what does your uncle say to you?'—'He says nothing to me, nothing.'—'Well, then, what does he do to you?' 'He kisses me on the forehead, Sundays.'—'Are you afraid of him?'—'Ah, no, no; isn't he my godfather? he wouldn't have anybody but me bring him his food.' Perotte declares that he smiles when she comes; but you might as well say the sun shines in a fog; he's as gloomy as a cloudy day."

"But," I said to him, "you excite our curiosity without satisfying it. Do you know what brought him there? Was it grief, or repentance; is it a mania; is it crime, is it—"

"Eh, monsieur, there's no one but my father and I who know the real truth. My late mother was servant in the family of a lawyer to whom Cambremer told all by order of the priest, who wouldn't give him absolution until he had done so—at least, that's what the folks of the port say. My poor mother overheard Cambremer without trying to; the lawyer's kitchen was close to the office, and that's how she heard. She's dead, and so is the lawyer. My mother made us promise, my father and I, not to talk about the matter to the folks of the neighborhood; but I can tell you my hair stood on end the night she told us the tale."

"Well, my man, tell it to us now, and we won't speak of it."

The fisherman looked at us; then he continued:

"Pierre Cambremer, whom you have seen there, is the eldest of the Cambremers, who from father to son have always been sailors; their name says it—the sea bends under them. Pierre was a deep-sea fisherman. He had boats, and fished for sardine, also for the big fishes, and sold them to dealers. He'd have charted a large vessel and trawled for cod if he hadn't loved his wife so much; she was a fine woman, a Brouin of Guerande, with a good heart. She loved Cambremer so much that she couldn't bear to have her man leave her for longer than to fish sardine. They lived over there, look!" said the fisherman, going up a hillock to show us an island in the little Mediterranean between the dunes where we were walking and the marshes of Guerande. "You can see the house from here. It belonged to him. Jacquette Brouin and Cambremer had only one son, a lad they loved—how shall I say?— well, they loved him like an only child, they were mad about him. How many times we have seen them at fairs buying all sorts of things to please him; it was out of all reason the way they indulged him, and so folks told them. The little Cambremer, seeing that he was never thwarted, grew as vicious as a red ass. When they told pere Cambremer, 'Your son has nearly killed little such a one,' he would laugh and say: 'Bah! he'll be a bold sailor; he'll command the king's fleets.'— Another time, 'Pierre Cambremer, did you know your lad very nearly put out the eye of the little Pougard girl?'—'Ha! he'll like the girls,' said Pierre. Nothing troubled him. At ten years old the little cur fought everybody, and amused himself with cutting the hens' necks off and ripping up the pigs; in fact, you might say he wallowed in blood. 'He'll be a famous soldier,' said Cambremer, 'he's got the taste of blood.' Now, you see," said the fisherman, "I can look back and remember all that—and Cambremer, too," he added, after a pause. "By the time Jacques Cambremer was fifteen or sixteen years of age he had come to be—what shall I say?—a shark. He amused himself at Guerande, and was after the girls at Savenay. Then he wanted money. He robbed his mother, who didn't dare say a word to his father. Cambremer was an honest man who'd have tramped fifty miles to return two sous that any one had overpaid him on a bill. At last, one day the mother was robbed of everything. During one of his father's fishing-trips Jacques carried off all she had, furniture, pots and pans, sheets, linen, everything; he sold it to go to Nantes and carry on his capers there. The poor mother wept day and night. This time it couldn't be hidden from the father, and she feared him—not for herself, you may be sure of that. When Pierre Cambremer came back and saw furniture in his house which the neighbors had lent to his wife, he said,—

"'What is all this?'

"The poor woman, more dead than alive, replied:

"'We have been robbed.'

"'Where is Jacques?'

"'Jacques is off amusing himself.'

"No one knew where the scoundrel was.

"'He amuses himself too much,' said Pierre.

"Six months later the poor father heard that his son was about to be arrested in Nantes. He walked there on foot, which is faster than by sea, put his hands on his son, and compelled him to return home. Once here, he did not ask him, 'What have you done?' but he said:—

"'If you do not conduct yourself properly at home with your mother and me, and go fishing, and behave like an honest man, you and I will have a reckoning.'

"The crazy fellow, counting on his parent's folly, made a face; on which Pierre struck him a blow which sent Jacques to his bed for six weeks. The poor mother nearly died of grief. One night, as she was fast asleep beside her husband, a noise awoke her; she rose up quickly, and was stabbed in the arm with a knife. She cried out loud, and when Pierre Cambremer struck a light and saw his wife wounded, he thought it was the doing of robbers,—as if we ever had any in these parts, where you might carry ten thousand francs in gold from Croisic to Saint-Nazaire without ever being asked what you had in your arms. Pierre looked for his son, but he could not find him. In the morning, if that monster didn't have the face to come home, saying he had stayed at Batz all night! I should tell you that the mother had not known where to hide her money. Cambremer put his with Monsieur Dupotel at Croisic. Their son's follies had by this time cost them so much that they were half-ruined, and that was hard for folks who once had twelve thousand francs, and who owned their island. No one ever knew what Cambremer paid at Nantes to get his son away from there. Bad luck seemed to follow the family. Troubles fell upon Cambremer's brother, he needed help. Pierre said, to console him, that Jacques and Perotte (the brother's daughter) could be married. Then, to help Joseph Cambremer to earn his bread, Pierre took him with him a-fishing; for the poor man was now obliged to live by his daily labor. His wife was dead of the fever, and money was owing for Perotte's nursing. The wife of Pierre Cambremer owed about one hundred francs to divers persons for the little girl,—linen, clothes, and what not,—and it so chanced that she had sewed a bit of Spanish gold into her mattress for a nest-egg toward paying off that money. It was wrapped in paper, and on the paper was written by her: 'For Perotte.' Jacquette Brouin had had a fine education; she could write like a clerk, and had taught her son to write too. I can't tell you how it was that the villain scented the gold, stole it, and went off to Croisic to enjoy himself. Pierre Cambremer, as if it was ordained, came back that day in his boat; as he landed he saw a bit of paper floating in the water, and he picked it up, looked at it, and carried it to his wife, who fell down as if dead, seeing her own writing. Cambremer said nothing, but he went to Croisic, and heard that his son was in a billiard room; so then he went to the mistress of the cafe, and said to her:—

"'I told Jacques not to use a piece of gold with which he will pay you; give it back to me, and I'll give you white money in place of it.'

"The good woman did as she was told. Cambremer took the money and just said 'Good,' and then he went home. So far, all the town knows that; but now comes what I alone know, though others have always had some suspicion of it. As I say, Cambremer came home; he told his wife to clean up their chamber, which is on the lower floor; he made a fire, lit two candles, placed two chairs on one side of the hearth, and a stool on the other. Then he told his wife to bring him his wedding-clothes, and ordered her to put on hers. He dressed himself. When dressed, he fetched his brother, and told him to watch before the door, and warn him of any noise on either of the beaches,—that of Croisic, or that of Guerande. Then he loaded a gun, and placed it at a corner of the fireplace. Jacques came home late; he had drunk and gambled till ten o'clock, and had to get back by way of the Carnouf point. His uncle heard his hail, and he went over and fetched him, but said nothing. When Jacques entered the house, his father said to him,—

"'Sit there,' pointing to the stool. 'You are,' he said, 'before your father and mother, whom you have offended, and who will now judge you.'

"At this Jacques began to howl, for his father's face was all distorted. His mother was rigid as an oar.

"'If you shout, if you stir, if you do not sit still on that stool,' said Pierre, aiming the gun at him, 'I will shoot you like a dog.'

"Jacques was mute as a fish. The mother said nothing.

"'Here,' said Pierre, 'is a piece of paper which wrapped a Spanish gold piece. That piece of gold was in your mother's bed; she alone knew where it was. I found that paper in the water when I landed here to-day. You gave a piece of Spanish gold this night to Mere Fleurant, and your mother's piece is no longer in her bed. Explain all this.'

"Jacques said he had not taken his mother's money, and that the gold piece was one he had brought from Nantes.

"'I am glad of it,' said Pierre; 'now prove it.'

"'I had it all along.'

"'You did not take the gold piece belonging to your mother?'

"'No.'

"'Will you swear it on your eternal life?'

"He was about to swear; his mother raised her eyes to him, and said:—

"'Jacques, my child, take care; do not swear if it is not true; you can repent, you can amend;

there is still time.'

"And she wept.

"'You are a this and a that,' he said; 'you have always wanted to ruin me.'

"Cambremer turned white and said,—

"'Such language to your mother increases your crime. Come, to the point! Will you swear?'

"'Yes.'

"'Then,' Pierre said, 'was there upon your gold piece the little cross which the sardine merchant who paid it to me scratched on ours?'

"Jacques broke down and wept.

"'Enough,' said Pierre. 'I shall not speak to you of the crimes you have committed before this. I do not choose that a Cambremer should die on a scaffold. Say your prayers and make haste. A priest is coming to confess you.'

"The mother had left the room; she could not hear her son condemned. After she had gone, Joseph Cambremer, the uncle, brought in the rector of Piriac, to whom Jacques would say nothing. He was shrewd; he knew his father would not kill him until he had made his confession.

"'Thank you, and excuse us,' said Cambremer to the priest, when he saw Jacques' obstinacy. 'I wished to give a lesson to my son, and will ask you to say nothing about it. As for you,' he said to Jacques, 'if you do not amend, the next offence you commit will be your last; I shall end it without confession.'

"And he sent him to bed. The lad thought he could still get round his father. He slept. His father watched. When he saw that his son was soundly asleep, he covered his mouth with tow, blindfolded him tightly, bound him hand and foot—'He raged, he wept blood,' my mother heard Cambremer say to the lawyer. The mother threw herself at the father's feet.

"'He is judged and condemned,' replied Pierre; 'you must now help me carry him to the boat.'

"She refused; and Cambremer carried him alone; he laid him in the bottom of the boat, tied a stone to his neck, took the oars and rowed out of the cove to the open sea, till he came to the rock where he now is. When the poor mother, who had come up here with her brother-in- law, cried out, 'Mercy, mercy!' it was like throwing a stone at a wolf. There was a moon, and she saw the father casting her son into the water; her son, the child of her womb, and as there was no wind, she heard BLOUF! and then nothing—neither sound nor bubble. Ah! the sea is a fine keeper of what it gets. Rowing inshore to stop his wife's cries, Cambremer found her half-dead. The two brothers couldn't carry her the whole distance home, so they had to put her into the boat which had just served to kill her son, and they rowed back round the tower by the channel of Croisic. Well, well! the belle Brouin, as they called her, didn't last a week. She died begging her husband to burn that accursed boat. Oh, he did it! As for him, he became I don't know what; he staggered about like a man who can't carry his wine. Then he went away and was gone ten days, and after he returned he put himself where you saw him, and since he has been there he has never said one word."

The fisherman related this history rapidly and more simply than I can write it. The lower classes make few comments as they relate a thing; they tell the fact that strikes them, and present it as they felt it. This tale was made as sharply incisive as the blow of an axe.

"I shall not go to Batz," said Pauline, when we came to the upper shore of the lake.

We returned to Croisic by the salt marshes, through the labyrinth of which we were guided by our fisherman, now as silent as ourselves. The inclination of our souls was changed. We were both plunged into gloomy reflections, saddened by the recital of a drama which explained the sudden presentiment which had seized us on seeing Cambremer. Each of us had enough knowledge of life to divine all that our guide had not told of that triple existence. The anguish of those three beings rose up before us as if we had seen it in a drama, culminating in that of the father expiating his crime. We dared not look at the rock where sat the fatal man who held the whole countryside in awe. A few clouds dimmed the skies; mists were creeping up from the horizon. We walked through a landscape more bitterly gloomy than any our eyes had ever rested on, a nature that seemed sickly, suffering, covered with salty crust, the eczema, it might be called, of earth. Here, the soil was mapped out in squares of unequal size and shape, all encased with enormous ridges or embankments of gray earth and filled with water, to the surface of which the salt scum rises. These gullies, made by the hand of man, are again divided by causeways, along which the laborers pass, armed with long rakes, with which they drag this scum to the bank, heaping it on platforms placed at equal distances when the salt is fit to handle.

For two hours we skirted the edge of this melancholy checkerboard, where salt has stifled all forms of vegetation, and where no one ever comes but a few "paludiers," the local name given to the laborers of the salt marshes. These men, or rather this clan of Bretons, wear a special costume: a white jacket, something like that of brewers. They marry among themselves. There is no instance of a girl of the tribe having ever married any man who was not a paludier.

The horrible aspects of these marshes, these sloughs, the mud of which was systematically raked, the dull gray earth that the Breton flora held in horror, were in keeping with the gloom that filled our souls. When we reached a spot where we crossed an arm of the sea, which no doubt serves to feed the stagnant salt-pools, we noticed with relief the puny vegetation which sprouted through the sand of the beach. As we crossed, we saw the island on which the Cambremers had lived; but we turned away our heads.

Arriving at the hotel, we noticed a billiard-table, and finding that it was the only billiard-table in Croisic, we made our preparations to leave during the night. The next day we went to Guerande. Pauline was still sad, and I myself felt a return of that fever of the brain which will destroy me. I was so cruelly tortured by the visions that came to me of those three lives, that Pauline said at last,—

"Louis, write it all down; that will change the nature of the fever within you."

So I have written you this narrative, dear uncle; but the shock of such an event has made me lose the calmness I was beginning to gain from sea-bathing and our stay in this place.

Addendum

The following personages appear in other stories of the Human Comedy.

Note: A Drama on the Seashore is also known as A Seaside Tragedy and is referred to by that title in other addendums.

Cambremer, Pierre
Beatrix

Lambert, Louis
Louis Lambert
A Distinguished Provincial at Paris

Lefebvre
Louis Lambert

Villenoix, Pauline Salomon de
Louis Lambert
The Vicar of Tours

About the Author

As part of our mission to publish great works of literary fiction and nonfiction, Colour the Classics Publishing Corp. is extremely dedicated to bringing to the forefront the amazing works of long dead and truly talented authors. Connect with us!

instagram.com/colourtheclassics

facebook.com/colourtheclassics

Milton Keynes UK
Ingram Content Group UK Ltd.
UKHW022038301123
433552UK00016B/835